Winnie-the-Pooh MEETS THE KING

First published in Great Britain 2023 by Farshore
an imprint of HarperCollins*Publishers*
1 London Bridge Street, London SE1 9GF
www.farshore.co.uk

HarperCollins*Publishers*
Macken House, 39/40 Mayor Street Upper,
Dublin 1, D01 C9W8, Ireland

Illustrated by Andrew Grey
Written by Jane Riordan

Copyright © 2023 Disney Enterprises, Inc.
Based on the 'Winnie-the-Pooh' works by A.A.Milne and E.H.Shepard

ISBN 978 0 00 860689 3
002
Printed in United Kingdom by Bell and Bain Ltd, Glasgow

This book is produced from independently certified FSC™ paper
to ensure responsible forest management.

For more information visit: www.harpercollins.co.uk/green

Winnie-the-Pooh
MEETS THE
KING

Jane Riordan • Andrew Grey

Farshore

'Is it safe?' asked Piglet anxiously, as they stepped carefully on board a boat that rocked this way and that on the water.

'Did I mention my sea sickness?' added Eeyore, the old, grey donkey.

'Yes, you did, Eeyore,' replied Pooh, 'several times. But this isn't the sea. This is **London** and this is the **River Thames**.'

'Quite so,' said Piglet, who hadn't been listening properly. He was concentrating on carrying a particularly large acorn that he had brought as an emergency snack for their trip to **London**.

But there was just so much to look at ...

There was a grand building with a huge dome at the top. It was called St Paul's Cathedral and it looked down on Pooh and the others, making them feel rather small.

On the boat went.

'The London Eye!' the other passengers said, nudging each other and pointing, but Pooh couldn't see an eye, only a huge wheel turning ever so slowly but always ending up where it started.

The next stop was theirs.

'Westminster Pier,' came the announcement.

As they got off the boat, Pooh started to feel worried. He had never seen so many people before. A friendly police officer smiled at all the visitors and told them to head toward **St James's Park**.

'That's lucky,' said Pooh. 'That is where Christopher Robin said *we* should go too.'

Before they left that morning, Christopher Robin had told them that if you were a woodland animal who wanted adventure in **London** then **St James's Park** was the place to go. It was just as green as the Forest, with almost as many trees and there was a lake with snowy-white swans swimming on it.

Near the swans stood a strange-looking bird.

'Hello,' said the pelican, for that was what she was. 'You must be here for the King.'

At this, the friends looked confused and so the pelican told them about the **King**, the palace, and all sorts of other things like Crown Jewels, orbs and sceptres. And when she had finished, they thanked her and continued on their way.

'Kings and crowns and whatnot? It sounds like something out of a dream or a fairy tale,' said Eeyore.

But just at that moment, the friends looked up and it was almost as if they *were* in a fairy tale. Ahead of them, through the trees they could see a huge, grand building with golden gates.

'A castle,' gasped Piglet.

'A **palace**,' gasped Pooh.

'With a flag on the top,' added Eeyore, admiringly.

By now the park had got a lot busier. A crowd of people was heading through it towards the castle or palace or whatever the building was, and the friends got swept along with it.

At least Pooh and Piglet did.

'Where's Eeyore?' asked Piglet anxiously.

They looked all around them, but Eeyore was nowhere to be found.

'We'll have to find a high-up place to look for him,' said Pooh. And really it was a clever idea for a Bear of Very Little Brain because it was the only way they'd be able to see where Eeyore was.

Ahead they could see a balcony. 'This way,' said Pooh and squeezing themselves between the bars of the rather huge gate, they went towards it.

As luck would have it, the balcony was decorated with great swathes of red fabric and by holding on tight to the golden tassels, they somehow managed to climb up to the very top. The thought of Eeyore lost in the crowd, grumbling and having his tail trodden on, kept them going.

And when they finally reached the top and clambered over the side a huge cheer went up from the crowd below them. Piglet was sure the cheering was for him, but it was then that they noticed some people joining them on the balcony ...

Standing almost close enough to touch was the real-life **King** with his wife the **Queen Consort**, and lots of other royal-looking people. High on the **King's** head was an actual crown, just like the pelican had told them. The King turned and looked at them. If he was surprised to see them there, it didn't show.

'Is that for me?' he asked, and Piglet realised that the **King** was pointing to his acorn snack. 'The best gift of all is something living,' continued the **King**, 'I shall plant it here in **Buckingham Palace Garden**. If I treat it kindly and look after it carefully, one day, an oak tree will give shade to the next **King** and all those who come after him.'

Piglet handed over the acorn and managed to whisper something that sounded a bit like this: **'Your Most Magic~y … Your Royal High~up~ness,'** which made the King smile.

'Seeing as you are so very high-up,' said Pooh bravely to the **King**. 'Would you be so kind as to look and see if you can find our friend. He's a bit old and grey, with long ears and he loves thistles.'

'He sounds like an excellent fellow,' smiled the **King**. 'Thistles are the national flower of **Scotland**, a place my mother, the late **Queen**, loved. Might that be him?' he added, pointing out across the crowds.

And there, marching around a glorious fountain was Eeyore. Well not just Eeyore, he seemed to have found himself some other four-legged friends. Never before had Eeyore looked so grand. Gone was his normal slightly sad and saggy plod. His nose was high, his eyes were bright, and his ears flew behind him in the wind as he marched with the royal horses in time to the band's music. And as he marched, the crowd clapped and waved flags.

'Three cheers for the King!' they cheered.

'And three cheers for Eeyore!' joined in Pooh and Piglet.

It turned out that the **King** was rather busy that day, but he was very interested to hear about the **Hundred Acre Wood** and, as he said goodbye, he promised to visit it one day. He suggested Pooh and Piglet took the staircase back down, which they all agreed was much easier than the way they had come up to the balcony.

In the courtyard in front of the palace they found Eeyore talking to one of the **King's** guards.

'Far too loud,' Eeyore was saying. 'But I'm happy to have led the way here.'

'Time to go home,' said Pooh, 'Piglet doesn't have his snack anymore and my morning honey seems a long time ago.' And so off they went.

When Pooh, Piglet and Eeyore arrived back in the Forest, Christopher Robin had called a special meeting.

'Head of the parade,' boasted Eeyore.

'A King ... with a real crown,' observed Pooh. 'You were right, Christopher Robin, about having an adventure in that park.'

'My haycorn ... growing in a royal garden,' added Piglet, who still couldn't quite believe it all.

And the others listened in silent amazement to the wonderful story of the **King's Coronation**.

'When I grow up,' Christopher Robin said, 'I think I'll be King.'

'I thought you were already,' said Winnie-the-Pooh, a little surprised.

At this, Christopher Robin stood up extra tall. 'Well, I suppose I am the **King of Here,**' he replied, proudly, 'but **There** is even bigger.'

'I see,' said Pooh, who didn't, quite. Pooh had very much enjoyed meeting the King and talking about trees and other favourite things they had in common, but to Pooh, Christopher Robin was the most important person in the whole world and that's just the way it should be.

Did you know?

King Charles loves to **paint.**

King Charles loves dogs and used to own a Jack Russell Terrier called **Pooh.**

King Charles now owns all the whales and dolphins in the waters around the United Kingdom. They are called the **"fishes royal".**

There are more than 700 rooms in
Buckingham Palace!

King Charles is a qualified diver
and has explored the wreck of
The Mary Rose, which was
King Henry VIII's ship!

The **pelicans** in St James's Park
were gifted to the previous
King Charles (II) in 1664.